This is the story of Raymond,

an ordinary dog who, for a while,
led an extraordinary life.

For Abel, Elijah, and Alba

First U.S. edition 2017

Library of Congress Catalog Card Number pending
ISBN 978-0-7636-8950-6

APS 22 21 20 19 18 17
10 9 8 7 6 5 4 3 2 1

Printed in Humen, Dongguan, China

This book was typeset in Avenir.
The illustrations were created digitally.

Candlewick Press
99 Dover Street
Somerville, Massachusetts 02144

visit us at www.candlewick.com

RAYMOND

Yann & Gwendal Le Bec

CANDLEWICK PRESS

Raymond was a happy dog.

He was a good dog, too.

He said *please*—**"WOOF!"**

And *thank you*—**"WOOF! WOOF!"**

And he never complained,

even when getting his fur trimmed

by the doggy groomer.

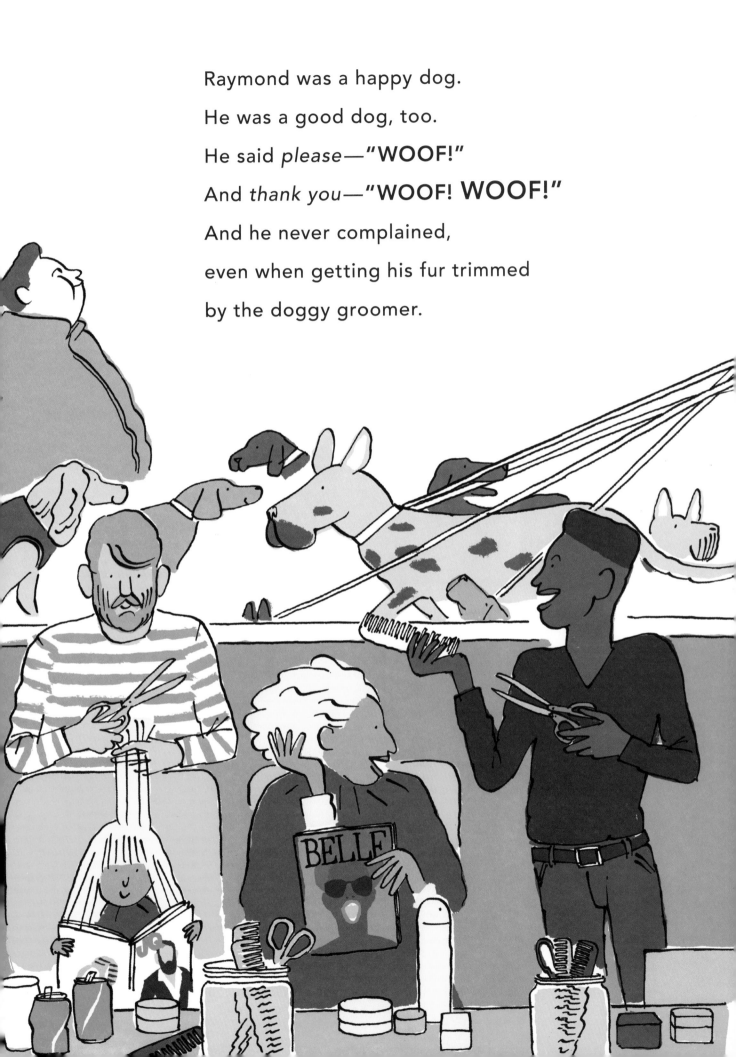

Raymond loved his family.
And they loved him, too—very, very much.
They always saved him a snug little spot
by the sofa, scratched behind his ears in just
the right place, and, every year, threw him
a surprise birthday party.

It was a pretty nice life for a dog.

But, one day, Raymond had a thought
(a rather **BIG** thought for a dog).
Looking up at his family seated around the
table, and looking down at his bowl of food,
he wondered,

Couldn't I just sit at the table?
Isn't that what families do together?

With each passing day, Raymond began
to act more and more like a human.
And, soon, so did every other dog in town.

There were cappuccino-and-cupcake Saturdays
at the café and trips to the movies
for action films and popcorn.

The world looked different on two feet,
bigger on two feet.

Raymond felt like he could do anything.

And that was when he spotted
DOGUE magazine.

Raymond felt as if **DOGUE** had been written just for him:

NEW WAYS TO SURPRISE THE MAIL CARRIER!

HOW TO AMBUSH CATS!

THE BEST DOG FOOD IN TOWN!

ALL THE LATEST DOGGIE FASHION NEWS—
"COLLARS OUT, SUNGLASSES IN."

So when Monday came, and Raymond watched his family

head out for the day, he had another (rather big) thought. . . .

"You're looking for a job, eh?" said the editor in chief
of **DOGUE** magazine.

"Yes, please," Raymond said, nodding.

"OK. So, tell me, what's your opinion on cats?" he asked.

"Well . . . they are *unbelievably* silly," said Raymond.

And the job was his.

Raymond became a full-time **DOGUE** rover-ing reporter and each day brought a new adventure.

He interviewed pooch painters . . .

top dog sniffers . . .

acrobatic poodles . . .

and tail-wagging tycoons.

Raymond was a very good reporter.

He pushed himself to meet deadlines,

working, always working,

to sniff out the next big headlines.

Even at night,
all his family could
hear was Raymond
tap-tap-tapping on
his computer.

He worked himself
to the bone.

Before long, Raymond became the face
of the biggest dog TV channel around,
Dog News.

His family tuned in every night;
it was the only time they got to see
their Raymond.

Soon, *everyone* wanted a piece of Raymond.

His fur wasn't just trimmed—it was washed,
combed, and styled every single day.
It was all becoming a bit too much.

WHAT A DOG'S LIFE.

For his birthday, Raymond's family
finally persuaded him to take a break.

But the whole way there,
Raymond couldn't help panicking
about the work piling up—
the phone calls . . . the e-mails . . .
the meetings . . . his FUR!

Until . . . a ball went *bounce bounce bounce* right by him.

And Raymond felt a familiar feeling.

A feeling he had forgotten all about . . .

HE JUST HAD TO CHASE THAT BALL!

WOOF!

He had forgotten how **MARVELOUS** it was
to have his belly scratched!

And what fantastic fun it was
to get his paws dirty!

A DOG'S LIFE WAS ABSOLUTELY BRILLIANT!

And, back home, as Raymond cozied

up in his snug little spot,

he decided that work could wait.

There were much more important things to do.

Like getting your ears scratched

in just the right place.